CW01604354

The Topiary Cat

A Bushy Tale

by

Richard Saunders

Surrealist

Richard M Saunders
'THE MASTER'

Dedicated to my family
and beloved Tolly

The Topiary Cat - A Bushy Tale by Richard Saunders
First published by Art Van Go Publishing *November 2021*
The Studios, 1 Stevenage Road, Knebworth
Hertfordshire SG3 6AN
Distributed by Art Van Go www.artvango.co.uk
Printed and bound in the UK by BookPrintingUK
Remus House, Coltsfoot Drive
Peterborough PE2 9BF
Telephone: 01733 898102
Website: www.bookprintinguk.com

Copyright © 2021 Richard Saunders
All rights reserved. No part of this publication may be reproduced, stored in a retrieval system, or transmitted in any form without prior written permission of the publisher or the author. For permissions contact: art@artvango.co.uk or surrealmoustache@gmail.com The right of Richard Saunders to be identified as the author, illustrator and photographer of this work has been asserted in accordance with the Copyright, Designs and Patents Act 1988. Cover art, illustrations, photographs, typesetting and design by Richard Saunders.
'The Topiary Cat' logo is sole copyright © Richard Saunders

ISBN 978-0-9573511-3-4
Edition 200

www.thetopiarycat.co.uk

CONTENTS

The Topiary Cat: *an introduction*

Welcome to the fantasy world of The Topiary Cat. This awesome being has lived with us for over ten years now, beginning as a single image that I made just for fun. I had taken a photograph, in the grounds of an historic house, of a huge cloud topiary, and it occurred to me that I could fairly easily photograph Tolly, our beloved Russian Blue cat, in a position to match the shape of the bushes.

The image was initially posted on Flickr, a photo-sharing website, but it was stolen and my name removed without my knowledge or approval. It turned up on a Facebook page called 'Amazing Places' and claimed to be a 'real' topiary. Thousands of hits were garnered from this post, none acknowledging my image creation.

Someone at the BBC noticed her mother looking at the image on her tablet computer, plus others I had made, and, intrigued, did a story for their online page. It then was shared worldwide, on Reuters and dozens of other news and blog outlets. One of the images (facing page), of The Topiary Cat drinking from a lake at Painshill Park, had over three million hits on my Facebook page, and The Topiary Cat website crashed due to the gigabytes of hits.

I have been a surrealist painter since I was a teenager and learned to use Photoshop over two decades ago in my job as an advertising Creative Director and Art Director. The idea of creating The Topiary Cat, while Tolly was still alive, was easily accomplished with skills I already knew. The images have become more complicated since, many taking days to produce, with tailor-made photos taken specially for them, often incorporating more than a dozen images. No deception has ever been intended, except by those who removed my name and misappropriated my copyrighted images, but the aim has always been to make them appear as real as possible.

The Topiary Cat has a life of his own on Facebook. There, I speak in the third person about 'The Master', myself, with whom 'TTC', his acronym, often disagrees and has arguments with on the page. The Topiary Cat's character is wise and brave, as was Tolly, but he doesn't understand human mortals.

Tolly died in 2016, and I was too upset to consider continuing with The Topiary Cat, but thousands of followers on Facebook persuaded me to carry on in his memory. It helps them when their own furry companions pass on, and during the Coronavirus pandemic it was a comfort and distraction for many of them for whom I created puzzles, 3D images and this novel, which I also read on YouTube, chapter by chapter, and then transferred it to SoundCloud. So The Topiary Cat's adventures continued. He is now accompanied by another much-loved Russian Blue called 'Georgi' who at the time of writing this is three years old. His topiary alter ego in the images is rather misbehaved and is called 'GK' (Georgi Kitten) by his topiary mentor.

In this book you'll discover the reasons for The Topiary Cat's superior nature, why he doesn't understand such simple human concepts such as time, or such odd human preoccupations such as 'working', 'school', 'weekends' or 'telephones'.

Richard Saunders – June 2021

The very first image of the altered cloud topiary bushes that become known as 'The Topiary Cat', first posted on 'Flickr' in 2010.

The photograph of beloved Tolly, Richard's Russian Blue, taken for the above montage.

The Topiary Cat

A Bushy Tale

by Richard Saunders

The 'Richard' in this story is semi-autobiographical, based on my recollections of the village I lived in, Much Hadham in Hertfordshire. The 'Grandpa' is also based partly on me, though I have little talent as a topiarist. Some of his interests are similar, and I am indeed called 'Baba' by my granddaughter. I also lived in 'Baba's house', the small flint cottage that was once a school, with my mother, Katie, who named the house 'Tara'. She had red hair and was artistic, as is her character in the book.

Richard's mother, Katie outside 'Tara' in the 1960s.

Just to help you remember who's who, here are the main characters:

Richard: *Nine and a half years old, a shy freckled lad*
Tolly: *Richard's companion, a brave, intelligent Russian Blue cat*
George Oakley: *Richard's Grandfather, called 'Baba' by Richard*
Katie: *Richard's mother, artistic, redhead, intelligent divorcee*
Colonel Edwin Greenwood: *Ex-Military, owns Neffertam Hall Estate*
Bastet: *Egyptian Cat God, intimidating and magical*
Doris: *Owner of the local newsagent and confectionery shop*
Snowball: *Doris's large white cat: fat, fluffy and lazy*

Chapter One:

WHERE WE MEET GRANDPA AND RICHARD

"Where are you?" shouted the old man. 'I bet I know where you are!' he thought to himself. Stooping down by an impressive hedge, he saw the young lad crouching under the branches with a grey cat at his side.

"Hi there, you two! Still hiding away from the world I see. I've come to see your mummy. Is she writing her poems or painting again?" "I think so, Baba", whispered the preoccupied boy. 'Baba' was Richard's name for his grandfather. He couldn't pronounce 'Grandpa' properly when he was a toddler, and the name stuck. The cat appeared to nod in agreement, but maybe that was Grandpa's imagination.

Baba strode towards the run down cottage, rang the bell and disappeared inside, leaving the two chums to continue their games. The boy had made a small pyramid of sticks and was pretending to be Davy Crockett, a hero of his that he'd seen at the cinema. He imagined himself to be the

'King of the Wild Frontier', seated round a campfire with Tolly, his loyal companion. The fact that this sidekick was actually a cat didn't bother him at all.

In fact Tolly was an ideal playmate for a young fellow such as Richard. This Russian Blue cat was wiser than any other cat they knew, and seemed to understand this very shy lad's need for company. When Richard was only a few years old, his mother had bought the cat as a companion for her son. Her husband had left them, having decided married life with a young child was not for him.

Grandpa worked as Head Gardener in the big house up the road. His daughter, Katie, was artistic and forgetful, so Baba would often call in to see if she was looking after herself and her boy.

This time he had called in to offer help. The huge unkempt hedge in the front garden was getting a bit out of hand. And he had a plan…

At the stately home where he worked, Grandpa was famed for his topiary. The vast estate was full of his most amazing sculpted bushes: pyramids, spheres, peacocks, spirals and even strange figures. Some were created from box hedges, some from yew, and others from common or garden privet. There was even a great dome of a variegated holly tree which was magnificent and a huge cloud topiary on the approach to the house.

Baba had noted the bond between the quiet boy and Tolly. Something special was going on and Baba sensed this. He resolved to create something to honour this strangely touching friendship.

Tolly was the perfect subject. However he wanted this topiary to be just for Richard, and luckily that hedge behind the low brick wall in the front garden was the perfect starting point. But he was going to make this a surprise, and anyway, he wasn't absolutely sure he could capture Tolly's unique character in sculpted foliage.

He had seen Katie's sketches of the boy's furry friend and thought they would be perfect reference for a topiary sculpture. It wasn't hard to persuade her to part with a couple of her drawings. He just said he loved them and would like a couple to frame for the sitting room of the lodge where he lived nearby. This was at the entrance of the drive to Neffertam Hall.

So he simply told Richard's mother that he was "Just going to trim that hedge for you, it's looking a bit untidy".

Tolly was scampering back to the boy in haste...

Chapter Two

TOLLY HAS A FRIGHT

Meanwhile, Richard and Tolly were getting a bit bored with that game of cowboys and Indians, and had decided to go on an adventure. This elegant, intelligent feline with the knowing green eyes followed the child around, more like a dog than a cat, and was quite willing to explore with him.

They lived in a village in the country, surrounded by beautiful countryside, largely unspoiled. There were fields with a profusion of wild flowers, where bees would hum and butterflies flutter by. Even a skylark might make a tuneful appearance, while the village pond would seethe with frogs and tadpoles in the spring.

The companions made their way to Neffertam Estate which was only a short walk away. Richard loved to visit the gardens and admire Baba's topiary, and fortunately, being related to the head gardener, nobody at the big house minded them exploring there, as long as no parties or posh visitors were expected that day.

They decided to go down to the big ornamental lake, because this always seemed a magical place. The gazebo, a small Palladian building by the water, had a hidden attic room with a tiny round window, where the boy could gaze out and dream.

Tolly stayed outside, seemingly wary of climbing the narrow stairs. Richard watched as he prowled about pretending to stalk some imaginary prey. Stopping for a moment beneath one of the many stone and marble statues, the one of Leda and the Swan, Tolly seemed to be looking directly into the eyes of the mythical princess. Then something extraordinary happened, or at least, Richard was convinced it had. The head of the statue turned towards the cat and, yes, the lips appeared to be moving. No, it cannot be! He blinked and looked back at the scene.

Tolly was scampering back to the boy in haste, as if something important was happening. The statue now looked entirely immobile. Richard rushed down the narrow stairs, nearly tripping over himself in his hurry. He scooped Tolly up in his arms and found that the cat was trembling.

"I wish you could talk, Tolly!" he said. "Whatever's the matter?"

Tolly nuzzled up close to the boy's neck and remained there while they made their way home. When they arrived at the front gate they saw Grandpa had begun to clip the hedge. "You won't destroy my hidey-holes will you, Baba?", cried the boy in alarm.

"Of course not, Richard, I know how much you love this hedge, I'm just trimming it. It's become a bit untidy, that's all!"

Tolly stayed with Richard all evening, never leaving his side. When it was time for bed, the cat followed him up the rickety stairs. This was most odd behaviour, usually Tolly was out all night getting up to adventures on his own.

Everything about their home was wonky, because it was centuries old and had been built using ship's timbers for the frame. Up a slope to bed and down a hill to the loo.

Chapter Three

BABA'S SURPRISE

Richard dreamt that night, as he often did. He was very good at dreaming, it was his own special talent. In fact he spent much of his time practising it, even during the day.

This time a particularly lucid dream woke him. The statues at Neffertam Hall had all come to life, surrounding him and Tolly, jabbering away incoherently in a most disturbing fashion. He woke up sweating and agitated. Katie had heard his groans and rushed upstairs. She took his temperature and it was higher than it should be. There would be no school tomorrow, for which he was grateful, as he didn't enjoy it much.

He was not a sickly child, but did succumb to influenza and the usual childhood ailments. This time it was definitely the 'flu. His normally pale face was even paler than usual and his freckles looked like the spattered paint on his mother's smock.

He stayed in bed for over a week, mostly reading. He liked books, especially those with fantastic stories and lots of pictures to fire his

imagination. Tolly would come up and snuggle down on the bed with him, sometimes crawling under the bedclothes and sleeping soundly there in the comforting warmth.

When he was feeling a little better he rose shakily from his bed and wandered to the window overlooking the front garden. Blearily, he peered out at his beloved hedge and rubbed his eyes in amazement. That was certainly his hedge, but transformed magically into a giant dark green … Tolly! It was so like his constant companion that he stared unbelieving at this apparition. Was he still dreaming?

Baba! Of course, this was Grandpa's doing. He surely was The Master of Topiary.

When Richard had fully recovered from his influenza and allowed to go outside with Tolly, he was able to appreciate fully the majesty of this sculpted marvel made from leaves, twigs and branches, expertly trimmed to shape. His secret hideaways had been carefully kept, with the entrance now decorated with a delightful leafy gothic arch.

Chapter Four

CLEVER TOLLY

It was a little while before Richard remembered his disturbing adventure with Tolly at the gazebo by the lake. Perhaps he had imagined it all, being caused by the start of his ’flu? After all, he had a similarly worrying dream when his fever took hold.

He determined to try and forget about it, though the memory of his troubled companion trembling in his arms was harder to dismiss. Being only nine and a half years old, such things don’t bother children of that age for long. Soon he was out and about with Tolly, hiding under his newly sculpted hedge and having exciting adventures as if nothing had happened.

It wasn’t until they revisited the lake one afternoon after school that the bothersome memory returned unbidden. Tolly looked a bit nervous too, so they stayed away from the statue and the gazebo, and wandered over to the formal rose gardens with their immaculately trimmed box hedges that bordered the flower beds. Marble statues of Greek, Roman and Egyptian gods were dotted around and box pyramids punctuated the low borders.

When they were wandering along the paths they noticed a problem with the neat box hedging. It was covered in brown and bare patches! Tolly sniffed suspiciously at the sad-looking bushes and his hackles raised. This wasn’t right.

Richard looked at the statue of Rodin’s ‘Thinker’ and sensed that it was pondering the problem. Even the statue of Hermes had a worried expression, whilst Aphrodite looked positively alarmed. Is the garden dying? Is that what Leda was trying to tell Tolly that day by the lake?

Grandpa was working in the huge greenhouse in the grounds that day, so Richard headed in that direction, Tolly dutifully trotting alongside. There, Baba was tending a raised bed full of young plants.

"Hello, young Richard – and Tolly too! What brings you here?"

"We've seen the bushes in the rose garden and they look sick! Have you seen them?"

"Yes, indeed. I'm afraid it is box blight. But it doesn't kill the plants and I have my team ready to cut out the affected areas. Don't worry, they will grow back!"

At this Tolly became distressed and began to miaow piteously. You know that saying 'He understands every word you say!'? Well, that's what it seemed to Richard and Baba. The anxious cat seemed to be trying to lead them back, tugging at Richard's shoelaces and pulling him back to the hedges by the rose beds.

This strange behaviour prompted the pair to follow the agitated animal to where he was leading them. Back by the box hedge, Tolly's nose pointed to something that the gardeners had missed before. It was a caterpillar, greenish-yellow with a black head.

"Tolly, you clever kitty!" said Grandpa. "Earlier I assumed it was box blight but now I see it is Box Tree Caterpillar! We shouldn't get this pest here, it comes in from imported plants and I know better than to bring them to our gardens. It must've been brought in with the last batch of young box plants that came in. We will have to pick them all off by hand."

"Why don't you just spray them Baba?"

"I don't want to spray insecticide, it might kill insects we do need. Thank you so much, Tolly, but how on earth did you know?"

"I think I know how, Baba. But if I told you, you wouldn't believe me!" Richard smiled to himself.

Richard imagined that he had discovered the mysterious link between this miraculous cat and statues, for he thought that was how Tolly knew about the problem of the dying box plants.

However, that night, lying in bed pondering the day's events, he began to doubt himself. Tolly had been seriously upset, shivering with what appeared to be fear after the statue confronted him. Surely a sickly plant would not have made him so fearful, would it?

Chapter Five

BABA AT HOME

Next morning wasn't a school day, so the boy was able to do pretty much whatever he liked. After breakfast of a boiled egg and toast, he looked outside for Tolly, his faithful friend. Mummy was always busy with her painting and poetry, so left him to his own devices. Dad was long gone, and Richard had few regrets. They didn't get on; his father was strict and Richard was 'wilful'. Now, Grandpa was a different character altogether. Richard loved him to bits.

He resolved to visit him at his little flint lodge. Richard knew Baba wasn't working today either, though he was aware that, even on Grandpa's day off, he often went to the gardens to trim the hedges. He was a bit of an obsessive regarding his topiary creations.

Tolly was easily found. He was waiting for Richard under the sculpted hedge which looked so very much like this beautiful blue-grey creature, it was uncanny. In fact, sometimes, when Tolly was off hunting, the boy would talk to The Topiary Cat in the same way he did to his furry friend. Richard ducked under the low entrance, his head brushing the leafy arch. He had always been a bit tall for his age, which simply made him attempt to hide away more. He picked up Tolly, and with the cat held snugly against his chest, headed off towards Baba's home. They passed between the imposing gateposts, each crowned with a carved sphinx.

Richard always thought Grandpa's home was an enchanting place to live. It was tiny, but very tall, with diamond-patterned windows. The many small panes of ancient distorted glass glittered and created wonderful reflections on the walls inside. The front door, a solid affair with huge cast iron fittings, seemed way too big for the diminutive property.

Raising the elaborate knocker, which sported an unsettlingly lifelike grimacing face, he let it go with a resounding 'clunk'. The reassuring sound of shuffling feet and a slight grunt announced the presence of his

old relative. Tolly craned his neck forward in anticipation, then relaxed as the door creaked open.

"Richard! What a nice surprise, and lovely Tolly too. Come in, come in!"

"Cup of tea and a bikkie?" Baba had a quirky approach to language, loving wordplay and puns. 'Bikkie' was what he called biscuits, or 'cookies' as they are known in the USA.

He opened an ancient and beautifully decorated hexagonal tin. Inside was a mouthwatering array of biscuits in assorted colours and flavours. There were chocolate bourbons, pink and cream wafers, iced gems and minty-green sugar-coated round ones with a hole in the middle. The bewildering choice didn't stop Richard for one second. He was looking towards Baba's larder. Grandpa looked up to the ceiling and snorted. He knew what Richard really wanted: a marshmallow filled, chocolate coated teacake, wrapped in glittering foil. He always chose them, and Baba knew it, he was just teasing the lad.

"And Tolly? What shall we give you, ay? Ah, I know…"

He disappeared into the kitchen and returned with some tiny scraps of cold chicken. He knew the cat was well fed and not likely to be hungry but always appreciated a little treat when visiting. Loud purrs confirmed his assumption.

"Baba. I have a question. What could make a cat so scared he was trembling like a leaf when I picked him up?"

"Oh, many things can frighten a cat. You're talking about Tolly though, I guess, and he doesn't scare easily. He's a brave pussycat. Dogs maybe, foxes, badgers. I've not been aware of any instances locally myself. Had he just had a fright when you picked him up?"

Richard was reluctant to relate his adventure with the statue, in case he was thought silly and merely imagining things. But Grandpa was a man with a vivid imagination too, and quite open to extraordinary events.

So the lad recounted what he thought he had seen. Baba went very quiet, listening attentively. After he had heard the story, he looked very thoughtful and a slight frown clouded his features.

Chapter Six

THE MYSTERY DEEPENS

"Well, that is quite a tale, isn't it? And, do you know, I believe you. I've been seeing strange things in the rose garden myself. There's something going on with the statues that has disturbed me as well. When I'm there in the early morning, or just before I go home in the evening, I often imagine I have seen movement out of the corner of my eye. But until you told me about Tolly just now, I had dismissed it."

At the mention of his name, Tolly looked up from his chicken treat and mewed softly. Behind his green eyes, Grandpa swore he could see a glimpse of matters far beyond the knowledge of mere humans. He knew that cats had a sixth sense and he imagined it being of great use, if only we could access it.

"Let me show you something, Richard." Baba led Richard to the loft and dropped a ladder down. "Stay there, Tolly!", the boy said, as the cat put a paw on the bottom rung. Grandpa flicked a light switch on and led the way.

When they had clambered through the small hatch, Richard could see Baba's telescope pointing through a narrow window in the end wall. Grandpa went over to a desk nearby and pulled a newspaper out of a drawer. "I've been noticing odd star alignments recently and so have other amateur astronomers. There's an article in the newspaper about it." Richard took the paper. The headline was 'A new constellation appears, puzzling astronomers'. "What's a 'constellation', Baba?"

"It's just a pattern of stars, Richard. See my star chart on the wall? There's 'The Great Bear', 'Cassiopeia', 'Andromeda' and so on. Some of them look like animals, others are named after gods because of the shapes they suggest. Remember when you came up one night and we looked at the moon and Saturn's rings? I also explained how two galaxies could collide without one star hitting another, and you found that hard to understand. I also pointed out Orion, a hunter in a Greek myth; now that's a constellation."

"I thought those had been there for ever, and you couldn't get 'new ones'?"

"Well, that's what everyone believed. Until now. It is very, very odd indeed. The newspaper has marked the locations of the 'new' stars in the sky, but nobody has come up with any theories yet as to what they might signify. I had done a sketch of my own before I saw theirs, you can have it if you like. Now we had better go down, your mummy will be worried if you're away too long."

"Hmm, she won't!", Richard thought to himself. His mother was probably too engrossed in her art to be aware he was out. He preferred it that way; he wouldn't have wanted her to be worried and, being a sensible lad, he was very careful. He wouldn't talk to strangers – he was too shy anyway – and he knew how to cross a road safely.

On the way home, Tolly by his side, he mulled over the conversation with Baba. It was all very confusing. These events: the statues, Tolly's reaction and the mysterious stars appearing, all seemed to be linked, but how? He clutched Baba's star sketch tightly, resolving to study it that evening in his room.

Passing through the front gate, he looked up at The Topiary Cat, serene in the evening sunlight. 'The Topiary Cat looks so wise I can almost see him thinking!' he thought to himself. Really Richard wished the bush could talk, but he didn't dare tell this to anyone, they thought him odd enough already. Spending hours with Tolly, making up stories, gazing into a pond, or just looking up at the clouds and seeing faces and animals in the shapes, was considered strange behaviour by less imaginative souls.

After dinner, he rushed up to his room and laid the star map out on his desk. Tolly sat right next to it, and, unusually for a cat, didn't sit on top of the drawing, but gazed at it fixedly just as Richard was doing. The dots Baba had marked on the sheet were clear enough; he had drawn them quite large in black with the other stars smaller in blue ink.

After staring at the dots for a very long time, the boy yawned loudly, stretched and shuffled across the creaky floorboards to bed. Tolly lay on top of the covers in a tight ball and went straight to sleep. He seemed reluctant to go outside hunting at night again. Richard switched off the light and was astonished to see an unusually bright after-image of the star chart imprinted onto his retina. Laying in bed looking up, it seemed as if the stars were actually there in the sky above him and the ceiling had flown away. It was indeed a jaw-dropping sight, but soon Richard's eyelids began to droop and he nodded off into a deep sleep.

Chapter Seven

REVELATION

Next morning, Richard awoke with a start. "That's it!" he cried. He must tell Baba. The star pattern now seemed obvious to him, and he was kicking himself he hadn't recognised it earlier.

"Where's Tolly? Mummy, have you seen Tolly?" No, she hadn't and she told him that the cat had attempted to wake him earlier but the boy had been too heavily asleep to stir. Tolly had gone out, leaving some of his breakfast which he usually wolfed down to the last scrap.

Richard told Katie he was going to look for the cat. Neither were particularly concerned. Tolly was an independent cat and not a 'homebody' like many of his breed. Often he'd be gone all day, only returning for dinner and then disappearing again. The lad strode off purposefully in the direction of Baba's lodge.

When he arrived at the front door, there was Tolly staring up at the door knocker, as if puzzling out how he could get it to make a sound. It seemed he had tried scratching at the door.

Richard knocked loudly, waiting for the familiar noise to come from within. It was still quite early, and, it being a Sunday morning, surely Baba was home. But no, no sound came. Was the old man ill? Richard looked through all the windows and the curtains were drawn back, so Grandpa had already been up that day. That was reassuring.

'He's probably gone to tend his precious topiary!' thought Richard. So the two chums headed off to Neffertam Hall again, and sure enough there was Baba, talking to a couple of his gardeners. On a Sunday? But, wait. What's this? Some of the statues had been placed together facing one another in the centre of the manicured lawns in front of the house.

"Baba, Baba! Are you okay, and why have you moved the statues, and what's going on? I came to tell you I think I know what the stars look like and…"

"Woah there, young Richard, settle down! I'm as confused as you are. Peter, go on telling us what you saw last night."

"Well, as I were saying, I couldn't sleep and were looking out me window in the early hours when I thought I saw movement 'ere. I were looking across the lawn and I swear I saw the statues moving in the moonlight! As the marble sculptures are valuable I thought it were robbers. But, I couldn't see any people and the statues appeared to be moving by themselves. I couldn't believe my eyes. I rubbed them and looked again. Everything seemed normal. So I went back to bed and thought no more of it, convinced it must've been a dream. When I looked out this morning the statues were 'ere, so I rang you boss, and we come over to investigate."

Richard looked at the statues. They were arranged in a tight group, all facing one another as if deep in conversation. He could see no movement and, looking down, the grass appeared undisturbed. The gardeners continued talking animatedly among themselves and Baba was so engrossed in their conversation that the boy decided his news would have to wait, especially as Colonel Greenwood was going to be informed.

The head gardener's job was much more important than Richard's revelation at this moment, so he and the cat wandered over to where the statues should have been. He expected to see tracks, or at least some disturbance to the ground. But no: where each figure had stood the bases were clean and unmarked, the soil around them still neatly raked.

He made a mental note of the names of the figures carved on the plinths. There were six gods in all: Jupiter, Gaia, Demeter, Neptune, Venus and Helios. He wasn't sure what they all represented, apart from recognising some planets among them. He would talk to Grandpa later, but the fact that celestial bodies were involved was quite interesting in light of his recent theory.

Chapter Eight

A DISCOVERY

Tolly was acting oddly again. When the pair had enough of reading the carvings, the cat seemed very eager to move on. This time he was heading to an area of the huge estate which the boy had always tried to avoid, but now felt impelled to follow. It was in the woodland, and much overgrown with brambles and nettles. Hathor Wood also had a reputation for being haunted.

The guests didn't go there either. The house and gardens, where the posh people had their parties and lived a life ordinary folks could only dream about, were scrupulously maintained but there was so much that it was too vast a job for a few gardeners to manage. The whole estate covered many acres and was hundreds of years old. Some of it hadn't been fully explored even now.

The task of bringing the gardens back to life after the war fell to Grandpa twenty years ago. He delighted in rooting out the original plans from the attic in the big house, with their beautiful illustrations made by garden planners so long ago. It was slow, painstaking work but extremely rewarding. When plans were too faded or illegible he was allowed some artistic licence, so where it simply stated 'Topiary Bush' in a caption, he could use his imagination freely.

Following the cat was becoming exceedingly arduous now and with gathering gloom and a threat of rain, Richard was becoming a little concerned. He was also getting a bit scratched by thorns and stung by nettles. Something about Tolly's mood made him carry on despite his misgivings, but nevertheless he was relieved when the cat halted, sat down and looked first ahead, then at Richard and then back again.

It was indistinct, covered in foliage and very dark, but there in front of them, surrounded by the remains of a cobbled area, was a large mound with a heavy wooden door cut into its side, almost obscured by brambles. This must have been there for centuries as there were trees sprouting from the top with roots extending down the sides like protecting arms. They approached the ancient door, Richard warily, the cat more confidently. To Richard's surprise, Tolly squeezed through a gap in the rotted timbers. The boy became very concerned at this. His precious cat had entered a ramshackle looking construction that appeared ready to fall down. He was now desperately worried Tolly might get trapped in there. He would have to go in and make sure the cat was all right.

Richard, heart beating furiously, gripped a heavy iron door handle. With a little effort, he managed to open the door enough to slide inside sideways. He could see more there than he expected due to a skylight, which, although covered with dead leaves, let a glimmer of light through. Tolly was sitting again, this time in front of a short flight of stairs leading downwards. As soon as Richard was inside, the cat abruptly shot down the steps, so now the boy felt compelled to follow.

With some trepidation, the nervous lad, summoning up every ounce of courage, descended the steps to discover a narrow dimly lit tunnel. This must have been only a few feet under the woodland floor and had thick glass roof lights at intervals, albeit also covered in roots and débris from the trees above. He could see alcoves on both sides of the path set into the walls, but as he had no torch he couldn't see very much and anyway he was too scared to peer in. Who knows what might be lurking in there?

The cat was now striding confidently ahead, with some speed. He obviously knew where he was going, even if the young master didn't. The passage sloped gently downwards which Richard found a little disturbing, but something about his beloved cat's demeanour encouraged him to continue this bold adventure.

After some yards the tunnel became more twisty so one could not see so far ahead. After yet another bend in the path Richard could see a slightly lighter area, which turned the image of Tolly into a silhouette. His cat was now sitting down, staring straight in front of him.

Emerging into the light, Richard took stock of his surroundings. It was a circular room bathed in light, a bit like the geodesic domes he had seen in the illustrated encyclopaedia Grandpa bought him last Christmas. All round the circumference was a stone bench. Looking up, he was startled to see fish swimming above his head. Where on earth had the pair arrived? Richard thought for a moment about the direction in which they had travelled and it dawned on him. They must have been heading towards the ornamental lake, the place where Tolly had been so disturbed by the statue a few days ago.

Now, however, something else caught his eye which made him even more excited; the sculpture on the round dais in the centre of the dome, which had also transfixed Tolly. It was a bronze representation of a cat, much bigger than a lion, but adorned with decorative jewellery such as those that he had seen in illustrations of Egyptian cat gods. Even more extraordinary was another simple fact, plain for all to see. The constellation that Richard had imprinted on his eyes last night was exactly the same shape as this statue.

Richard could see an inscription on the platform upon which this magnificent beast stood. It read 'Bastet, Egyptian Goddess of Cats, Defender of the Innocent, Avenger of the Wronged'. What was surprising was that, unusually, the cat was not depicted as seated as he had seen in his books, but striding forward with an expression in her eyes that he found not a little disturbing.

He picked Tolly up and headed rapidly back up the increasingly gloomy tunnel to the mound and out into the woods beyond. In spite of this extraordinary discovery he wasn't keen to spend long inside there, something felt threatening about it. Outside in the fresh air, there was now a howling wind and driving rain. He hurried home, not even stopping to find out what had happened with grandpa and the statues. Sometimes a lad just needs his mother.

Chapter Nine

GRANDPA & THE COLONEL

"I have to see Grandpa again, mummy. There are odd things happening in the gardens up at Neffertam Hall. Is it all right if I go there now? I haven't any homework today and I do have important things to tell him." Katie was quite easy to persuade and Richard had already had a cup of tea and a piece of cake. "Don't be late for dinner though, Richard!" she shouted after him. "Seven o'clock sharp!" She was joking of course, the boy had no sense of time passing, so she nearly always had to keep his food warm for him.

It was still afternoon when he arrived at the hall, so he was convinced Grandpa would be working. He couldn't see him in the grounds so he headed towards the estate office, noting on the way that most of the statues had been replaced and the last one was being lifted back onto its plinth using a fork lift truck. He usually found such pieces of machinery irresistible, but this time he was impatient to see Baba.

When he arrived at the small wooden estate building, he held back. It was crowded with people: some uniformed police officers, a few of the gardeners including Peter, and the commanding figure of Colonel Greenwood. Richard found him rather intimidating, being very tall with a bushy moustache and a military bearing. He also had a booming voice which seemed to carry for miles.

Richard could hear that voice clearly from yards away. "Well, you lot had better keep a watch on this place then, hadn't you? It must have taken a number of strong men to get the statues that far. And you tell me you didn't hear a thing, Peter? Extraordinary. I want this sorted out before Falcon, or else."

The policemen looked somewhat abashed too, having also been reprimanded by the Colonel for dereliction of their duties. This was most unfair, but typical of this ex-military man. He had no time for shirkers or anyone who didn't do exactly what he expected of them, even if they had not been directly ordered to do so. He demanded initiative, self reliance and total loyalty from his employees. To be fair to the Colonel, he was actually very concerned. He felt he was merely the custodian of Neffertam for future generations and honoured to be in a position to restore it to some of its former glory.

When the small crowd had dispersed, leaving Baba alone at his desk, Richard ventured inside. Grandpa looked up, but his look was not quite as kindly as usual. He looked older and more tired too.

"Oh, hallo, Richard" he sighed. "I'm up to my neck in work at the moment. The truck has made deep furrows in the lawn and damaged some of the rose bushes. We have to sort that out before the weekend, there are important guests coming to stay for Falcon. I still don't know what's going on, and now on top of all that, we are going to have to set up a night watch in case the thieves return."

Richard looked downcast. He felt whatever he had to say had receded in importance compared to Baba's problems right now. Whatever had this 'falcon' thing got to do with anything? However he had noticed some old sepia photographs on Grandpa's desk that looked interesting. They were obviously very old indeed and quite faded, including images of the garden showing features that had now been lost.

"Baba, I can see you're very busy, so I shan't bother you now. Is there any chance you could lend me those photos? I think there may be something there that could help us to find out more about these mysteries." Baba was only too happy to send the boy away with the photos, he knew how careful he would be. He put them inside a thick leather-bound folio for protection and, after a short lecture on their historical importance, sent the boy on his way.

Katie was startled to see Richard return well before dinner but not so surprised when he rushed up to his room, barely acknowledging her on the way. Tolly was already in Richard's room, fast asleep on the bed, having spent a long day hunting animals that didn't wish to be caught. He was exhausted and probably rather miffed at his failure to catch any tasty rodents. Richard laid the precious photos out on the desk and began to study them with a magnifying glass.

Note: In the centre of the image above, 'Baba's House' is actually the Victorian building in Much Hadham that the author lived in during the sixties. The photograph shows when it was being converted from a school to a domestic building. The grand manor house just above it is 'Hadham Towers', photographed by the author just before it was, sadly, demolished to make way for gravel pits. It was designed by the architect Charles Fitzroy Doll as his personal residence. Here this dilapidated manor represents 'Neffertam Hall' in a state of decay.

Chapter Ten

SECRETS OF NEFFERTAM HALL

Richard loved looking at old photographs. He felt he should have lived decades ago when life was simpler. He thought early Victorian times would have suited him better, with all those wonderful inventions to be discovered and fantastically elaborate architecture. He chose to ignore, or didn't know about, the hardships and deprivations of life in those days, unless one was born with money and power.

Some of the photographs appeared to be from that period, before the estate fell on hard times. There were a few images obviously from wartime: rows of wounded soldiers seated, with young women standing behind them in smartly pressed nurses' uniforms and a heavily built severe-looking matron stood to the side.

What really excited Richard though, were some old photos of the grounds of Neffertam Hall. It was clear that Baba had copied the plans to make the formal beds, but seeing them here showed just how skilled he and his team had been in recreating them. Richard immediately pounced on a photograph of the entrance to Neffertam Hall showing Baba's flint lodge. This was captioned 'The Sphinx Gates'.

To Richard, the most interesting image was one taken in the woodland he had visited yesterday.

There was the mound, showing clearly the doorway he had entered with Tolly. It looked so different then, because now it was covered in brambles and topped by sycamore trees. In those days it was surrounded by a cobbled area, with decorative inserts made from slate and terracotta that looked like huge snakes. There was a wide clearing around it and a brick path leading up to it. The most astonishing thing to Richard was that the earth mound was faced with flint around the entrance much like Baba's extraordinary home. However it must have been neglected for so long that nature had reclaimed it now.

What caught Richard's eye was an inscription above the doorway cut into the wooden arch. He peered closely through his glass and could just discern some of the letters.

'BEH_ _D _HE EY_ _F RA. BAS_ _T PRO_ _CT US'

This was frustrating, he couldn't make out any complete words at all. Was the first word 'behind' and the last but one 'product' or 'project' perhaps? It was a puzzle all right. He copied the lettering onto a piece of paper but it made no sense to him at all. He shuffled through the photos again and stopped at an image of a bronze statue. It was very like the one in the underwater dome, on an identical circular plinth. Yet this creature was seated in the classical regal pose we normally associate with Egyptian cat gods, not marching on all fours.

He longed to talk to Baba now; he knew everything, or so it seemed to the boy. Surely he would be able to decipher the carved lettering? He wondered if he knew about the strange building in the woods and the passage leading to the watery home of a magnificent statue. He decided to visit the library after school next day and do some research on his own.

Chapter Eleven

CONNECTIONS

It wasn't long after he had made his decision when his plan became unnecessary. After he and Tolly had their dinner that evening, there was a knock at the door and there was Grandpa.

"I've come to see Richard, Katie. He told me he'd discovered something about stars I had been looking at through my telescope that I hadn't seen before. And now they are getting brighter and brighter."

Katie looked perplexed. She didn't read the newspapers or follow world events at all, she was so focussed on her art projects. But now she was interested. Very interested indeed. She rushed to her makeshift studio in the back room cluttered with frames and unfinished works. She returned, holding up a colourful painting.

“Look at this! I had a sudden inspiration a couple of days ago, and just had to make an image of it!”

Astonished, Baba and Richard stared at the painting. Against a rich cobalt blue background was an array of stars surrounding a large disc of bright yellow. She had captured the glow perfectly to indicate this was the sun, but what struck the pair was that two snakes were wrapped around it. The obvious markings on the heads indicated that these were cobras. In the foreground in thick black paint was Tolly, instantly recognisable, silhouetted against the fiery disc.

The old man sat down with a thump onto a sofa. Richard stood there gawping. Neither knew what to say, then began talking excitedly at the same time. Katie looked puzzled and mildly alarmed at their reaction. “What’s going on, you two?”

Baba recounted what he knew about recent events and then asked Richard to tell them what he had discovered too. After he had related his experiences with the dream and the scary adventure with Tolly, he produced the paper upon which he had written the inscription over the ancient door. “Any idea what this says, Baba?”

“Yes, I think I can guess. You told me that the bronze statue was Egyptian and I know a bit about the history of that civilisation. The words are all to do with the gods of ancient Egypt.” He took Richard’s paper and asked Katie for a pen. Very carefully he began to fill in the blanks. When he had finished, he sat back in the sofa and waited for a reaction, with a barely discernible smile of satisfaction. He didn’t like to appear a show off but this time he felt justified, if only a little bit. This is what he had written:

‘BEHOLD THE EYE OF RA. BASTET PROTECT US’

“But what does it mean, Baba? What is ‘The Eye of Ra’ and what would Bastet be protecting?”

“Well, some of this is going to be guesswork. I am not all-knowing like

these gods were thought to be by the Egyptians! I've spent quite a lot of time trying to find out about the previous owners of Neffertam Hall. One thing that's become very clear is their obsession with cats, in fact I understand that over the centuries they owned dozens of them. I say 'owned' but, as you well know, cats are never really 'owned'. We are merely their slaves!"

Did Tolly prick his ears up at this? Richard was sure he had. In fact the cat was sitting up so attentively he almost expected him to join in the conversation, though quite what sort of voice he would have, the boy couldn't imagine. Baba continued.

"I think the mound you discovered in Hathor Wood was built to house the cats after they'd passed away. Possibly the inscription is urging Bastet to protect the spirits of the animals inside. I believe you saw alcoves along the tunnel? I'm guessing that is where the bodies of the cats are, and knowing how revered they were, I think they would have been in some sort of casket, each one marked with the animal's name."

"The whole construction of the mound you described could be a representation of the sun. 'The Eye of Ra' is, in myth, enclosed by snakes, specifically cobras. Bastet was the daughter of the sun god Ra. She was spirit guide for the dead in the afterlife. Now, Katie's painting is a clear reference to that as well, which is quite remarkable. All we have to do is find out why this is all happening now … and what it all means!"

They all sat back trying to absorb so much information. So many puzzling connections it made their brains swim. All this was new to Katie, and she didn't know what to think about the pair's revelations. So she stood up and said loudly:

" Right, you lot! Bedtime. It's late, I'm tired and I have to think. I expect you do too."

And, with a swish of her flame-red hair, she went straight upstairs, leaving Richard to say goodbye to Baba. They resolved to talk again soon, but Grandpa was still having to work all hours on the estate, getting ready for forthcoming guests that weekend. It occurred to Richard that his old friend must now be very tired, if he had been spending time peering through his telescope as well.

Note: This is Katie, Richard's mother in the story. The image is based on a photograph of the author's late mother, Cathleen Saunders, also known as Katie.

Chapter Twelve

A DISTURBING DREAM

That night, Richard fell asleep almost instantly, with Tolly snuggled close to his head, sharing the pillow. The cat had seemed anxious again. Did he sense something? The lad was sure he did and it was so frustrating not being able to communicate with him.

Later, in the early hours, Tolly was disturbed by Richard's heavy breathing and the occasional cry, seemingly of alarm. The cat pawed at the boy's chest but that didn't wake him. It was a warm night, so Tolly went out into the dark garden and slept under The Topiary Cat.

Richard was experiencing a most vivid dream. He was back under the lake in the glass dome, standing before the bronze cat. The fact that it was now alive and able to talk seemed unremarkable, especially as, unusually, Richard was quite aware that this was a dream. Bastet was angry and her hackles were up. She addressed the boy, much in the way that his mother did when reprimanding him, but so much more terrifying.

"I have awoken from a long slumber. Mafdet has told me that you mortals have been careless, and justice must be carried out. I have sent you a sign that you might be made aware of the consequences of your actions. I have watched for centuries. You have venerated cats just as you should and I had begun to be kindly disposed to you all.

Once I was a ferocious avenger, provoking awe and fear into you. Later, when you started behaving yourselves, I protected your homes from evil spirits and eased your mothers through childbirth. But now, it seems you have forgotten the wrath of Ra, and you ignore his terrible power. The gods of old have been told of your misdemeanours. Now, go!"

The sight of a large heavy bronze paw, with claws outstretched, coming down rapidly next to him with an almighty 'Clang!' made Richard wake with a start. He had knocked over the bedside table lamp and he saw his alarm clock, which he rarely used, glowing faintly from under the bed. He arose shakily, trying to remember his dream. He often forgot them once he awoke, so quickly he set down on paper what he could recall. Some of the words were beyond his comprehension. What was that peculiar name Bastet had used? 'Miffdat'. 'Madfet'? Something like that.

'Now, where's Tolly? He was sleeping close to me when I went to bed', Richard wondered. He looked out of the window and his head shot forward in surprise, banging uncomfortably against the glass pane. The Topiary Cat's foliage was pulsating as if it was breathing and it appeared that the mouth was moving too! Tolly was staring up at the sculpted head of the bush and his beautiful grey cat's eyes seemed to be brighter and more green than usual. The boy could swear they were talking to one another! "Now really, I am letting my imagination run away with me!" Richard scolded himself aloud, as he did quite often.

His rational self persuaded him that it must have simply been a breeze moving the bush. However when the weather forecast for his region came on the radio as he ate breakfast, it said that the day was still, with no wind expected. He didn't tell his mother of his dream or the animated bush. She was even more preoccupied than usual today, and, having left Richard's cereal out ready for him, was already painting.

Chapter Thirteen

STRANGE GOINGS-ON

It was a shame he had to go to school and his teachers noticed he was looking out of the window again. More than once he was shouted at to pay attention. Richard knew that his mummy wanted him to go to the grammar school and she was sure he was bright enough, if only he would concentrate on his studies. But he found it hard to do so, especially just now, when there were more exciting things going on.

He couldn't wait for the bell to be rung so he could be free again. Rushing home, he paused at the grocer's shop to buy some 'Sherbet Dabs' with his pocket money. The lady that owned the shop was as sweet as her confectionery but also a bit of a gossip. She knew Richard quite well, in fact they might be considered 'friends' by others in the village. This wasn't entirely the case, they were more 'acquaintances' really. But she had a heart of gold and felt slightly sorry for the boy: always on his own apart from the cat, and wandering about in a dream half the time.

"Did you hear of the trouble up at the hall, Richard? All sorts of strange goings on, I've been told. They've even had the police round!"

"Well, I know they think there's been some burglars after the statues, Doris."

"No, no. Not that! They set up a night watch because of that. A couple of the groundsmen took it in turns to patrol the gardens last night and they've both gone missing. The police and your grandpa are out looking for them. Not only that but the lake's turned to gold! And have you seen the local paper? Look!"

Among today's newspapers on the counter he could see a banner headline: 'Huge Cat Spotted in the County'. This rather amused Richard, because right there next to the pile of papers sat Doris's big white fluffy cat, Snowball. Obviously she was not the cat mentioned in the article, but the thought that she might have been made him smile. In the newspaper was an indistinct black and white image, snatched by an amateur photographer from some distance away. Richard had seen similar images before; such sightings occurred at regular intervals all over Britain – usually when there was little else for journalists to write about. However, this time he recognised a disturbingly familiar dark shape.

Richard knew Doris was likely to be exaggerating events, she always did. He didn't think she could make up such an odd tale, her imagination didn't run to such flights of fancy. A golden lake indeed! He didn't know what to do. Baba now had even more to contend with. His missing workers, a ruined garden and important visitors only days away. Richard felt he shouldn't bother his grandpa. He desperately wanted to find out more, but how?

He headed home only to find Tolly waiting for him by the gate. The cat ran up to greet him, purring and rubbing against his legs. Inside the garden Richard looked up at The Topiary Cat. That's odd, he thought. I'm sure the cat's head was pointing upwards when Baba trimmed it and it now looks as if it's facing downwards. Has a bough broken or something? He went through the arch and looked up inside the neck of the sculpted bush. No, no snapped branches or fallen twigs. Just as he was about to disappear into the house, he thought he heard a voice. Very soft, like wind in the trees. He shook his head, dismissing it as his imagination. But, no. There it was again. He stopped and listened intently.

"Richard. I need to talk to you."

The lad had no idea where this voice was coming from and looked around for someone who might have spoken. He looked down at Tolly who seemed unperturbed. There it was again, more insistently this time.

"Richard. I need to talk to you. I'm over here."

Richard wheeled around, for now he knew the direction the sound was coming from, though it was hard to believe. It was coming from The Topiary Cat!

Chapter Fourteen

THE TOPIARY CAT SPEAKS

Baba had made the topiary into the shape of a sleeping cat, with its eyes tightly closed. He was a very clever topiarist but couldn't work out how to make convincing open eyes from trimmed foliage. Richard stood open-mouthed before the huge green cat whose head was now raised right up, and a pair of glittering green orbs was staring straight at him. Tolly didn't appear in the least bothered but Richard backed away, flattening himself against the door of the cottage in fear.

"Don't be afraid, Richard. See? Brave Tolly knows I won't harm you. Come closer, so I don't have to shout out, though I am sure only you and Tolly can hear me."

Richard approached the huge topiary head warily. His pet was already sitting there, ears cocked. Now, the boy recognised the voice of The Topiary Cat: it was very like the scary voice in his dream last night, but more kindly.

"That's better. Let me take a closer look at you, I want to be sure you are the right mortal for my tasks." Richard felt that was an odd way to put things. Why was he a 'mortal' and whatever 'tasks' would he be required to carry out? If he was considered 'mortal', was The Topiary Cat 'immortal'? So many questions flooded his mind from a single sentence.

"I see you have many questions, Richard. But I need to tell you important things urgently, so wait and you will discover some answers. Please sit down."

Something about the commanding voice demanded instant obedience. Richard sat cross-legged in front of the awesome leafy beast.

"I know you are aware of recent strange events and have had unusual dreams. I am the cat goddess Bastet and these are all my doing. I have been awoken from my centuries' long slumber, and come to earth to warn mortal humans of the consequences of their misdeeds. I chose Neffertam Hall first because of its long association with cats. Now, because of you and your grandfather's unique abilities, I am talking to you through The

Topiary Cat. You and Tolly have such an unusually strong bond, I felt it should be so. I believe you have immense empathy."

'She does seem to use a lot of long words!' Richard thought.

"I am sorry if I speak to you with words you cannot understand. I am used to talking to gods in a different tongue. Apologies. I shall try to use simpler terms, I know you are very young." It seems Bastet could read the boy's mind.

"The first task I wish you to carry out is to help recover the lost souls in Hathor Wood. I know your grandfather is concerned for their safety. You must take Tolly so you can find the crypt again and take – 'Baba' I believe you call him? – there with you. Then I am sure he will understand how to find his men. Do that and return to me. I suggest you communicate with me after dark in future. I do not believe your fellow humans would understand if they saw you talking to me. Now go."

The boy's head was beginning to spin, this was all so hard to grasp. He was being told what to do by … a topiary cat? And yet, and yet, something about this all made sense to him. Perhaps this 'empathy' thing was how he could process what was going on? But he would now have to talk to Baba. The Topiary Cat had resumed its usual pose, exactly the same glorious form as originally created by his grandfather.

"Mummy, mummy, I need to talk urgently with Grandpa. I think I may know how to find the men that are missing. I can't explain how, I just do. Will you telephone him and let me talk to him, please, please?" The urgency and serious tone in her son's imploring voice persuaded Katie to pick up the receiver of the heavy black Bakelite phone and turn the dial with its familiar whirring. After what seemed ages, Richard was relieved to hear the receiver picked up with a 'click!' and Baba saying his phone number.

"It's Katie, dad. Sorry to bother you, I know you're very busy."

"Hello Katie, you don't 'phone me often. Why now? Is something wrong?"

"Dad, I have Richard here, and he is desperate to talk to you. He imagines he knows how to find your workers. Don't ask me how!"

"You had better put him on then, I am terribly concerned for their safety. I've been told there's a large cat on the loose, as big as a lion. I really don't believe it, stories like this pop up all the time. It always turns out to be a hoax or something harmless."

Katie passed Richard the heavy handset and the words tumbled out. He didn't mention The Topiary Cat, that could wait. He asked Baba to come to the woods with him and to bring a powerful torch, because they had to go into Bastet's chamber. Grandpa was sceptical, but was also convinced that Hathor Wood was a likely place where the men could have disappeared.

Katie was very concerned for her son's safety but Grandpa reassured her that he was convinced the rumours about the animal were unfounded. It was almost certainly just a large pet cat, but he would make sure Richard and Tolly were safe.

He knew he would never be able to find the chamber in the woods without them, so, reluctantly, Katie agreed. She put some sandwiches in Richard's satchel which he slung over his shoulder. He hadn't had his dinner and it looked as if they might be gone some time.

Chapter Fifteen

THE HUNT IS ON

When Grandpa met Richard and Tolly outside the lodge, the lad was surprised and slightly alarmed to see that Baba was clutching a shotgun. He had talked to the gamekeeper on the estate, and, despite not quite believing there was an animal on the loose, he thought it better to be safe than sorry. With Tolly leading the way, Richard and Baba crossed the ornamental park and entered the darkening woodland. The chill air in the spooky woods made Richard shiver, but Grandpa's powerful torch created a comforting pool of light before them, and now the moon was rising.

The cat's tail, with its curled tip, looked like a soldier's flag leading a march. Baba stamped noisily, treading down the bracken and brambles to make the boy's progress a little easier. It seemed further to the mound than it had in daylight, and it crossed Richard's mind that maybe Tolly had forgotten the way. While he was thinking this, however, the eerie knoll loomed in front of them. But what's this? The ancient doorway was smashed and lying on the cobbles, the hinges hanging off the frame. The trio stopped and surveyed the wreckage warily, but it was ominously quiet.

"I think we shall have to go inside and find out what's going on," said Baba, "maybe the missing men are there or at least we may find some clues."

With trepidation they crept in, down the short stairwell and into the tunnel, looking left and right into the alcoves. The old man stopped and shone his torch into one of them. Sure enough, inside there was a small blackened silver casket covered in cobwebs. Sweeping them aside with his outstretched hand, Baba could discern engraved lettering inscribed on the lid: 'Mekal. 1897-1912'.

"This cat must have been a fierce hunter, I reckon, Richard. But we'd better move on, those men of mine may need our help urgently. But we'll

come back when all this is over and document all these beloved cats. This really is fascinating!"

They set off briskly down the tunnel, with the boy expecting any moment to see the faint greenish glow from the moon shining above the lake, glimmering through the glass dome. But what they actually saw was an unexpected and very faint, sickly yellow light ahead. Even more shocking was the fact that the bronze statue of Bastet was nowhere to be seen.

"I think the lake's been contaminated, Richard. Probably run-off from something the neighbouring farmers are spraying their crops with. That's bad, bad for the fish and for us. But there's nothing to be done now, we'd better get on."

As the room appeared empty and no other clues were evident, he swung round and strode back up the tunnel, with Richard and Tolly having to run along behind to keep up with him. Once outside Baba began searching for clues outside the area of scattered cobbles. Abruptly he dropped to his knees, and shone his torch at the ground in front of him.

"Look, Richard! Paw prints, and large ones at that. How very odd. Maybe those rumours of a big cat on the loose are true after all. But, hang on, the ground is quite hard here and those prints are very deep indeed."

"Erm, Baba…" Richard ventured. "I know this sounds crazy, but what if… no, no, sorry…" He tailed off with embarrassment and blushed slightly.

"Go on Richard, I'm ready to believe almost anything today! There are so many mysterious things going on, one more won't hurt."

"Well. What if – and please don't laugh at me – the Bastet statue has come to life, broken through the door and gone off into the woods?"

Baba almost began to splutter a laugh, but stifled it, and then looked serious.

“Sorry, if I looked sceptical at first, Richard. But now I think about it, Peter thought he saw our statues move on their own. All the other weird stuff going on makes me wonder if these are some sort of supernatural events, all connected. Even the largest lion certainly couldn’t cause such deep paw prints. It would have to be a very, very heavy animal indeed to do that. Still, whatever is causing those prints, I guess we had better follow them. I hope it leads to my lost men. Now, stay close behind me and I’ll keep the gun ready, just in case.”

The paw prints were leading them deeper into the heart of Hathor Wood. Fortunately the ground here was only covered lightly with leaves; the bracken, brambles and nettles that hampered their progress up until now having thinned out considerably. Then, they heard noises up ahead. A heavy rhythmic thump, thump, thump and what sounded like an angry voice and cries of alarm.

In front of them, in a small clearing, was the most extraordinary sight. Bastet, the bronze cat from the glass dome, was prowling in a wide circle around two men, who were crouching in terror before the beast.

Instinctively, Grandpa raised the shotgun to his shoulder and, when the animal was nearest to him, fired a shot. The pellets pinged off the metal cat harmlessly and the trio ducked to avoid the rebounding shrapnel. The creature whirled around to face them.

“Ha-hahaha! How amusing you mortals are, thinking you can harm an immortal god, you pathetic creatures! I and my cohorts have come here to warn you, not hurt you.”

She gestured, with a dismissive paw, to the two cowering men. “I have been trying to get these two silly mortals to hear me, but they are too stupid to understand.” Sitting down on her haunches, towering over Grandpa, she adopted the classical pose that befitted her status as an Egyptian god. Richard noted that her jewellery looked even more magnificent than ever, glittering in the moonlight.

Glancing briefly at Richard and Tolly, her features softened. Bastet continued. "I have met you two before, but is this your grandfather? I wanted to speak to him because he might just be able to comprehend the import of what I have to say. Otherwise I fear there will be dire consequences. Sit!"

Richard immediately recalled his conversation with Bastet in the form of The Topiary Cat. This time the same commanding instruction invited no dissent. It was an order without the magic word 'please' which Richard was always being reminded to use.

The three adventurers sat obediently and listened attentively to this awesome cat. The reason for these mysterious events was becoming clearer with every word spoken and, when her lecture was complete, she appeared satisfied. With a final warning of the fate that would befall them if they didn't do her bidding, she disappeared into the woods with a

Is this an ancestor of The Topiary Cat in ancient Egypt? We think so.

contemptuous flick of her magnificent tail.

When she had gone they all rose shakily and began to head back to Neffertam Hall. Baba asked his workers what had happened to them before they arrived on the scene.

"We was patrolling the grounds when we saw movement in the woods. We followed a crashing sound like heavy footsteps and we thought it might be the thieves we suspected of tampering with the statues. We ended up there in that clearing. Then this weird cat appeared and began circling us. It didn't seem as if it was going to do anything except keep us in this one spot. So we crouched down and, we couldn't believe it, but it started talking to us, like it was just now. But we couldn't make out what it was saying at all. It was obviously very important but made no sense to us whatsoever. You all seem to understand though! Why would that be?"

Richard thought for a moment and then piped up. "Baba, what is 'empathy'? I have been told you and I have this, but I don't know what it means!"

"It means that you have sympathy or an affinity with other living beings. Why do you ask – and who said we have it?"

"Erm, I really don't want to say where I heard it just now, Baba! But maybe that is why we understand what Bastet was telling us?"

"Could be, I suppose. It certainly seemed absolutely clear to me what she was asking for and what we have to do about it as well. I think your mother, you, me and of course, Tolly, should get together urgently and discuss our next move. I think all of us could do with a good night's sleep, I know I could. I'll come over tomorrow morning before you head off to school."

Grandpa turned to the bemused men. "Look, I know you chaps have had a bit of a shock but perhaps you could hold the fort for me tomorrow, but keep this to yourselves for now. I'll be back to Neffertam well before lunch. We still have lots to get ready for those visiting V.I.P.s."

The men wandered off grumbling to each other that nobody would believe them anyway.

Chapter Sixteen

MAKING PLANS

Sure enough, the following morning Baba arrived very early, having 'phoned Katie to warn her of the importance of their proposed meeting. She was excited at the prospect, because she too, had been receiving odd, almost telepathic, inspirations that seemed eerily relevant to current events. She had spent most of the last couple of days capturing them in paint.

Richard had risen at first light, and after breakfast he went back upstairs to keep a look out for Baba's arrival. Tolly sat by him on the windowsill. Looking over to The Topiary Cat, the boy wondered if he had imagined the conversation with Bastet, when she was disguised as Grandpa's trimmed foliage. It had seemed so real, but now he could see no change from the original topiary. Except, except… was that a slight kindly smile on the sculpted face? Ah, here's Baba.

"We'd better go down, Tolly." But his cat had already padded downstairs, anticipating Grandpa's arrival even before he was seen by the boy. Everyone knows cats can do that of course, but Richard was always amazed by this ability.

When he arrived downstairs the first thing Richard became aware of was an array of paintings taped to the walls of the sitting room. His mother had been busy! There were cats, in fact a great number of cats, pyramids, hieroglyphs, stars, birds of prey, bare trees and random shapes that were hard to decipher. A confusing jumble of symbols, images and figures but arranged in such a way, and in the most glorious intense colours, that they were staggeringly beautiful. Each of the assembled gathering told their wondrous tales to the others, who reacted with increasing astonishment and incredulity. It was only when they had all said their piece, that it made some sort of sense.

They all agreed that the most sage counsel had come from the terrifying cat in Hathor Wood. This bronze cat had always been The Sentinel of Neffertam Hall, just one of Bastet's many observers on Earth. She had warned her mistress of the presence of poison in the lake, and felt something had to be done urgently. The Bastet goddess told them that she had brought the statue to life, channelling her mind through the statue to warn mortals of the consequences of their actions.

She had discovered mortals were becoming careless with Mother Nature. In and around the estate, species were being introduced that should not be there, trees cut down with no thought to the repercussions, crops sprayed in farms nearby that killed beneficial insects and so much more. Other gods: Jupiter, Gaia, Venus and many others, had come down to inhabit their images on earth, investigate the problems and discuss among themselves what should be done.

They had searched for mortals they believed could address the problems, and Bastet had singled out the quiet boy, with his kindly grandfather and talented mother as likely candidates to spread the word. It was obvious they loved nature and the bounty it provided. So, Bastet had inhabited various inanimate images to get her message across, and it had certainly worked with some. She had become aware that many humans, including those unfortunate men in Hathor Wood, were less receptive to her demands. But she also knew that this was an especially propitious moment to spread the word, because Mother Nature was fighting back.

Grandpa was going to have to talk to Colonel Greenwood urgently to see if something could be done about the damage being caused to Neffertam Hall Estate and the neighbouring countryside. None of them could guess what the consequences of inaction might be, but they were surely not about to risk finding out.

She had discovered mortals were becoming careless with Mother Nature.

"Now, come along Richard, you'll be late for school," his mother interjected, bringing them all down to earth with a jolt. The boy had, in his excitement forgotten all about school!

He rushed upstairs for his satchel, crammed the cap onto his head and ran up the road at top speed so as not to be late for assembly.

Chapter Seventeen

EXPLANATIONS

Back from school, Richard could hardy wait to see what events had happened since he left. Tolly was there waiting by the gate again and led the boy straight to The Topiary Cat. Would the lad's sculpted bush talk to him again, he wondered? The giant green cat didn't stir at first, not until Tolly mewed softly. The Topiary Cat seemed to wake from its reverie and looked down at the pair with benevolent eyes.

"Ah, there you are, young master Richard, with brave Tolly at your side, just as it should be. I hope the task I set you didn't scare you too much. You and your grandfather did find the missing men."

"Oh, yes, thanks to you! We had such an adventure, and we met the bronze cat in Hathor Wood too and we…"

"You don't need to tell me what happened Richard, I was there, speaking to you through the bronze sculpture in my image, just as I am doing now with your topiary cat. You, your grandfather and your mother are key to all this. The tasks I shall set you are of utmost importance. I shall have to speak to 'Baba' again soon. I have already spoken to your mother today."

"What! You talk with mummy too, Bastet?" Richard was a little disappointed at this, he would have liked to have kept the talking topiary cat to himself. It did however make life easier, because his clandestine chats would be a little less nerve-racking now.

"The missions I shall assign to you from now on are not so immediate Richard, nor so frightening. They are much more important and may affect your whole life. But it will not be easy and less empathic mortals may try to dissuade or even force you from pursuing them. Please tell your grandfather I wish to speak with him here urgently, before Falcon."

At last, he would be able to find out how a bird of prey could possibly be involved in these events.

"What is 'Falcon', please, Bastet? It's been mentioned before and I think it's something to do with the weekend isn't it?"

"I'm not aware of this 'weekend' thing, Richard. What is it?"

"Oh, well, erm…" Richard was perplexed. He had assumed Bastet knew everything and it was a bit of a shock that he had to explain to this amazing creature about something so ordinary as a 'weekend'.

He carried on as best he could, explaining to the bewildered green cat about 'going to work' and 'school' and the fact humans took a couple of welcome days off every five days. The Topiary Cat listened intently, then shook its leafy head.

"How strange! Humans never cease to astound me. Thank you for explaining that so clearly. Now, 'FALCON': it is what you mortals call an 'acronym'. The initials simply stand for 'Farmers And Landowners CONference', that is all. I need to speak to Baba before that happens."

"I'll let him know straight away. I'll get my mother to 'phone him." He could tell that the 'telephone' was another human concept that Bastet didn't really understand, but he let that go for now. He turned and had already headed for the front door, when The Topiary Cat called after him:

"By the way, Richard, why not call me 'TTC'? That is also an acronym, for 'The Topiary Cat'. I don't think you should call me by my goddess name, it is disrespectful and inappropriate for me in this guise."

Richard called out from the hallway, while he wiped his shoes on the mat by the door. "Mummy, mummy! I think you've talked to my topiary cat, haven't you?" Katie rushed to meet him in the hall, looking quite flustered.

"Yes, dear. I was out in the front garden doing a bit of weeding. I'd neglected it 'cos I was so busy painting. I was looking up at its face, because after what you'd told me I was curious to know if it could possibly be true. I couldn't believe it when those beautiful eyes opened and it spoke!"

She told Richard how friendly the giant cat seemed and showed pleasure that she was recording such momentous events through her extraordinary paintings. The Topiary Cat had urged her to show these works to a wider audience, so Katie resolved to hold an exhibition of her work and ensure that visitors would be aware of the motivation for the images. She neglected to mention that the green cat also said such lovely things about her son, that she glowed with pride.

"Mummy, The Topiary Cat wants to speak to Baba, will you phone him and let him know, please?'

Chapter Eighteen

PREPARING FOR FALCON

Grandfather was honoured to have been granted a personal dialogue with The Topiary Cat, and, despite being very busy working late at Neffertam Hall, made every effort to visit Richard and Katie that very evening. He desperately wanted to know exactly what was needed to avoid the possibility of further disasters at the estate.

It was late when he arrived at the cottage and dusk was falling fast. He glanced up at The Topiary Cat, but hurried on to the front door, resolving to have Richard alongside when they spoke together for the first time. For a second he became sceptical that his sculpture in foliage could possibly come alive; it looked just as he had created it a couple of weeks ago.

Richard appeared at the door almost immediately after Tolly. They gathered by the head of The Topiary Cat and waited but couldn't discern any movement from the green giant, so they looked quizzically down at Richard's grey cat. Tolly seemed in something of a reverie but hastily became alert, as if he had only just realised what was expected of him. He mewed softly. Foliage rustled and shook, and those vast green eyes opened once more.

The Topiary Cat rose up and sat in front of them, towering over them with a kind, but very serious, expression on those leafy features. Richard saw that his grandfather looked quite perplexed and obviously rather intimidated by his own creation behaving in such an extraordinary manner.

In fact Richard realised immediately that this was actually not a very good idea, because now The Topiary Cat was visible from the road, and, despite it being late evening, he was worried the locals might spot this incredible sight.

So he piped up, somewhat timidly, suggesting that TTC might consider settling back down into the original shape created by Baba. Fortunately

Bastet soon realised the common sense of the boy, and adopted a less prominent pose.

The Topiary Cat spoke at length to Baba, who listened attentively. Most of the instructions were straightforward, though complex to arrange in the short period before FALCON. Some tasks could be carried out soon afterwards, such as the cleaning of the lake and avoiding such contaminations in the future.

The most daunting thing to Grandpa was that he was directed to speak to the attendees of the conference on matters that some of them may not wish to hear. He wasn't at all sure Colonel Greenwood would let him speak there at all, and Baba was not used to speaking in public, let alone to a possibly hostile audience.

Later, Katie had something else to say to Baba, which involved another request of the Colonel, and this was quite a big thing to ask. "Oh, well," groaned Grandpa, "In for a penny, in for a pound!" Richard didn't follow his meaning but his mother certainly did.

Chapter Nineteen

THE POWERS OF BASTET

Next morning Richard's grandfather put on his smartest clothes and arranged a meeting with Colonel Greenwood. To his surprise and relief, the Colonel was remarkably affable for once. This severe man, who had been so stubborn and cantankerous in the past, had been chastened by previous events and could see his plans for Neffertam Hall jeopardised if he didn't implement some changes. If his head gardener was likely to ease the transition to a better future for the estate, why would he impede him? He certainly didn't think his estate manager, even though he was very competent at making the place profitable, had the vision this older man possessed.

Soon the Colonel was on the phone to the manager with clear instructions to change the running order of speakers, reprint the conference schedule and prepare the tithe barn, normally used for wedding receptions, for a last minute event.

At home after school, Richard made a real fuss over Tolly. This loyal and brave companion had been a treasure and delight in this extraordinary adventure, so extra treats and lots of cuddles were given to him that evening. Much later, out in the garden, they both sat by The Topiary Cat. Richard informed Bastet that the Colonel at Neffertam Hall was going to let Baba speak at the conference and she told Richard that she would make sure to be there in front of the building when the V.I.P.s arrived.

Richard sat bolt upright in alarm. "What? You're going to leave our garden, wander about the village and sit outside the hall? You'll terrify everybody and something horrible will happen. People do nasty things when they're confused and frightened!"

"Calm down Richard. I've thought hard about this, thanks to your sage counselling when I unwisely sat up yesterday evening. I have abilities far beyond mere mortals such as yourself. Don't forget, I am Bastet and have magical powers human minds cannot comprehend."

"I can change shape at will, assuming the appearance of topiary wherever there are suitable bushes to hide in. I will only move under cover of darkness, along hedgerows or through woodland. If I have no choice but to move during daylight, I shall only do so when no mortals are around. If unexpected people appear, I shall remain absolutely still and can camouflage myself with ease. Humans are predictable, they only see what they expect to see and few have an imagination as fertile as your own."

"But, but … won't someone notice you aren't in my garden when you wander about?"

"No, they will not, young man. Watch and I will show you." And with that Richard and Tolly watched in awe and disbelief as The Topiary Cat

got up and strode over to the far side of the garden with a loud rustle of foliage! Incredibly and confusingly, Grandpa's original topiary remained exactly where it was created. This one was different though. They could tell that no spirit occupied it, it was simply a wonderfully sculpted bush just as Baba had created it.

"How did you do that, TTC? I know you can do magic, but that is just … weird!"

"Ha-ha! You have no idea what miracles I can perform, have you? One day I shall tell you more of my secrets, but not today. Maybe your grandfather can guess, he has an inquiring mind and hates not understanding how things work. Ask him if he has any theories!"

With a swift farewell, The Topiary Cat padded stealthily into the night in the direction of the Neffertam Estate.

Chapter Twenty

THE CONFERENCE

The weekend dawned bright and clear, the gardens looked immaculate and the guests were beginning to arrive. The huge hedge by the house was a 'cloud' topiary with an indistinct abstract form, neatly trimmed. As the large chauffeur driven cars swept up the long gravel drive towards the hall, their passengers' eyes were inevitably drawn to this topiary. However to a few more perceptive visitors, it now appeared to resemble a magnificent sleeping cat.

The Topiary Cat was evidently keeping a very close watch on proceedings at the hall. Back at Richard's home, Baba's original topiary remained, inanimate and undisturbed.

The conference was a two day event. Saturday was devoted to guests settling into their rooms, a lavish luncheon followed by various light-hearted entertainments: a theatre troupe with jugglers, comedians and musicians, and for those who simply wanted to relax, the beautiful grounds to explore and admire. Various charities had set up stalls; it was an excellent fund-raising occasion for them.

There was also an art exhibition in the impressive tithe barn. This was a wonderful building with huge ancient timbers supporting a high vaulted ceiling. It was a sought after wedding venue for those who could afford to hire it. Large screens had been placed around with vibrant paintings hung on them.

Katie had been reluctant to sell them, so had put very high prices on them, hoping she would keep them. They were so personal to her, and to her father and son, she had put them on sale reluctantly, but the Estate Manager had insisted they should be for sale, with a percentage for charity. She had been able to display them so quickly because she used

the same size canvasses for all her works. Suitable frames were always stacked ready in her studio.

She hovered around nervously waiting for a reaction from guests who wandered inside the barn. A hastily prepared banner announced the title she had chosen for the show: 'Signs from Egypt'. It wasn't long before a prosperous looking lady came over to her and began talking to Katie animatedly. She adored her paintings and wanted to buy one. When told the price she didn't bat an eyelid, but wrote a cheque out there and then.

Word spread to the other guests of these glorious works and a regular stream of wealthy visitors ensured that her record book of sales was kept open all weekend. She took every opportunity to remind people of the message her paintings conveyed.

Meanwhile, Grandpa, who had to be on call throughout the weekend, was ensconced in the Estate Office trying to compose his speech for tomorrow's lecture. It wasn't easy: juggling pleas for care, admonishing transgressors, asking for assistance to reverse damage and understanding the needs of landowners to make a living while producing the food we all need.

He shouldn't have worried. The conference was deemed an astounding success with Grandpa's lecture a highlight. It was clear that many of the farmers and landowners had similar problems and had become concerned that Mother Nature was beginning to show her distress. Their use of poisons, creation of vast tracts of arable land devoted to a single crop, hedges uprooted and trees cut down, animals herded together inside buildings with no fresh air to breathe, no fields to graze or move around in freely, this was not a sustainable way to maintain the balance of nature.

There were of course a few sceptics who wouldn't listen, profit being their only concern. However, when the old man mentioned a book he had read recently, 'Silent Spring', and related the message it contained, most heads nodded with recognition.

The Topiary Cat heard all of this and was well pleased. Bastet knew she could return to her adopted home in Richard's garden knowing much of her task had already been completed. Her topiary disguise radiated such a glow of satisfaction that the foliage quivered noticeably.

Chapter Twenty-one

STARGAZING

While the conference was in progress, Richard had been dissuaded from going to Neffertam Hall. It wasn't seen to be appropriate to have a young lad wandering about unaccompanied with such important people around. So instead, he and Tolly spent most of the time together, simply enjoying the glorious weather, making up games and stories, and having adventures in the fields nearby. His mother had left him cold lunches, so he didn't go hungry. Of course he missed Bastet's company that weekend, but he was still able to play under the The Topiary Cat's welcoming shade.

After all the excitement and build up to the conference, it came as a welcome relief to everyone to have a little time to absorb and reflect on the extraordinary events of the last couple of weeks. Richard was glad that it was now holiday time. He found school an annoying distraction from these much more weighty matters. He was never very academic, but excelled at art and English. Little else interested him, though it wouldn't be all that long before he would have to take the 'Eleven Plus' and, if he passed enough exams, go to grammar school. He wasn't sure what he felt about that.

It was a couple of days before the adventurers managed to get together to recount what had been going on recently. Grandpa had been extremely busy co-ordinating the clean up of the lake and the surrounding farmland, and, with the estate manager's blessing, hiring heavy machinery and bringing in knowledgeable experts. Colonel Greenwood was overseeing operations and had been mightily impressed with Baba's grasp of the situation.

The family decided to have a celebration meal in Grandpa's home. He wasn't a very good cook and Katie never bothered much with fancy meals either, but all of them loved fish'n'chips. Every week a large van would arrive in the village and ring a loud bell to announce its arrival. This was

Bert's mobile chippy, serving delicious food to the neighbourhood. Most weeks Richard would be sent to get his and his mother's supper there at the top of the hill where the van stopped. This time the order was larger than usual.

"Hallo, Richard! You having visitors today? That's a bit more than you usually have, isn't it?"

"We're going to Grandpa's house today to celebrate! We've had a bit of luck."

The queue behind him, eager to give Bert their own orders, didn't allow him time to explain further, so clutching the comfortingly warm parcel wrapped in newspaper, Richard headed off for Baba's, Tolly joining him on the way past their cottage gate.

"Have a good evening, Richard. I need to talk to you tomorrow!"

Richard looked back, and up to The Topiary Cat, for he was sure it was Bastet's voice. The cat looked quite still, so he must have picked this message up telepathically. "Okay, TTC!" he shouted back.

Baba had set a table in the middle of the lodge's tiny sitting room, just big enough for three chairs, so they could sit and eat their meal together. They all had so much to say they couldn't wait to share their thoughts, so, just for once, Richard's mother wasn't too strict about her son's 'talking with your mouth full' behaviour or the fact that Tolly was being sneakily handed a few flakes of fish.

"The Topiary Cat wants to talk to me again, Baba. Bastet told me on the way here, at least I'm pretty sure she did."

"Yes, Richard. I'm not surprised. One or two guests came up to me after my lecture, saying they thought the topiary in front of Neffertam Hall had been re-trimmed by me into a large cat. When I said I hadn't, they either thought I was going senile or that they'd imagined it! Knowing what I

know now, I assumed Bastet's spirit inside the topiary was watching us?"

"I'm sure that's true. She said she was going to the conference to make sure everything went off OK. I didn't know exactly how she was going to do it, but that must be where she hid. I hope nobody thinks the bushes are alive, that would be hard to explain! I think Bastet wants to keep her secrets to herself, apart from us of course.

"Baba, Bastet told me that you may have an idea how The Topiary Cat could be in two places at once, then go back to being just one again?"

“Hmmm, maybe I can. Do you remember me telling you about colliding galaxies? How the stars looked so close together but in reality have space between that’s enough for them to pass through, without a single star hitting another? It’s a bit like that with atoms. They’re held together with energy but there’s more space than matter to them. Perhaps The Topiary Cat’s found a way to align the atoms in a similar way, so they don’t collide? Possibly that’s how Bastet does it.”

“I don’t think I completely understand, Baba, it makes my head hurt.”

“Well, there’s no need to bother about that now. When we’ve finished our supper, Richard, there’s something I want to show you and Katie. That constellation I told you about? You told me it looked like a prowling cat, just like the bronze under the lake. I was looking through my telescope last night, and it’s changed shape.”

After they'd had their cod and chips, Baba brought out a block of Neapolitan ice cream he'd bought at Doris's shop earlier. This was an unexpected treat, a luxury they only had on special occasions. It was Richard's favourite too, though he could never decide if he liked the strawberry more than the chocolate, or vice versa.

Up in the attic, Baba focussed the telescope, before urging Katie to take a look.

"I can see a few bright stars, daddy, is that all?"

"It's the shape they're in that's significant I think, Katie, and the fact that they weren't there until a month or so ago. Let Richard have a look now, he might spot something else that's quite remarkable."

Richard peered through the eyepiece, standing on a stool that Baba had thoughtfully provided for him. He pulled away, looked at Baba, then back again at the telescope, in disbelief. The constellation was a totally different shape and beginning to fade even as he watched.

"Baba, it's changed shape and it seems to be disappearing fast."

"That's right. I've been making sketches over the last couple of days, I cannot imagine what's going on. It is very interesting though!"

Richard took another look at the stars. They had nearly faded away, but were moving fast, creating an arc. They appeared to stretch and enlarge, becoming hazy and adopting many colours. Incredibly, he saw an image of a cat fly over it and disappear above the curved band into the black sky. Then the coloured arch vanished too, a flash of light and it was gone.

"Baba, it's gone! The stars have left and they made a sort of rainbow just before they went. And, and … I think Snowball has died!"

Grandpa and Katie stared at the boy. "Why on earth would you say that, Richard?" Baba said, shocked. "How could you possibly think you know that? I don't think that's true anyway. I was there buying the ice cream this afternoon and Snowball was there, grumpy as ever, but well enough as far as I could tell."

"I don't know, Baba. I just felt it. When I was looking at the stars I thought I saw a shape I recognised and, I just, well, I just … knew." He stumbled over this words, not understanding himself quite how he could possibly know, but he was certainly convinced he was right about it.

Grandpa looked to confirm Richard was right: that the constellation had indeed vanished, and it wasn't simply that the telescope had become knocked out of alignment. He had kept track of the stars' movements in a notebook which he handed to his grandson. Each page had been carefully traced over the previous one, so that Grandpa didn't need to plot all the existing stars over and over again.

Sure enough, over time, the shape the stars made altered subtly. From Richard's imagined 'prowling cat' it was changing into something else.

The expression 'couldn't make head nor tail of it' crossed his mind and he couldn't resist a smile. He thumbed through the pages again and again, then remembered the 'flick books' he loved playing with. Each page had a slightly different drawing of a cartoon character and when you flicked through the pages the figures appeared to move, just like an animated film. Now he knew exactly what the stars represented!

"I've got it, Baba! Please can I have a pencil?" He sat down at the desk and began to join the dots, then handed Grandpa the sketchbook. "Flick through the pages quickly, Baba, like a movie. See?" He showed Baba what he meant, gripping the spine of the book and using his thumb to flick through the pages.

Baba did what the boy told him and gasped with astonishment as he saw the crude image of a prowling cat stop, turn to the front and sit down, just as the bronze Bastet statue had done in Hathor Wood.

Chapter Twenty-two

SET TO RIGHTS

Next morning, Katie went to the grocer's shop to buy bread and eggs for breakfast. Doris was not her usual chirpy self, looking very distraught. When asked what was wrong she tearfully related how Snowball had passed away unexpectedly yesterday evening. The vet had been called and told her that the cat had been poisoned. He suspected the cat had ingested chocolate.

Doris was horrified, she had started giving her much-loved cat choccy treats, left a packet open and the greedy cat had wolfed down the lot. Katie knew better than to give chocolate to Tolly, she knew it could be fatal to cats. When Doris said that she was sure Snowball would be happy 'over the Rainbow Bridge', not something Katie had ever heard of, the explanation for Richard's extraordinary vision through the telescope became clear.

After breakfast, Richard went straight into the garden to talk to The Topiary Cat. Tolly was probably out hunting, so he wondered if TTC would respond to him alone. He had, up until now, assumed the giant cat would wake up only when Tolly mewed at him. He need not have worried, for the eyes opened and the topiary sculpture spoke immediately.

"Hello, young master. I am proud of you and your fellow adventurers. But there is one more important task for you. The owners of Neffertam Hall have neglected their traditional role, to maintain veneration of cats. They have no cats patrolling the grounds, their laps are vacant and their houses lack feline presence. The crypt has fallen into disrepair. It used to be a magnificent place, known widely and visited by admirers from around the country. The caskets are tarnished and forgotten, no candles are lit in the alcoves on St. Gertrude's Day and this makes all the cat gods angry."

"I'll talk to Baba, TTC. I know, I have seen for myself just how badly the place has been looked after, I was scared to go there. I wonder if Colonel Greenwood even likes cats though?"

"I shall visit him in a dream and make sure he understands the import of what I am telling you. I think I can persuade him, even if he's not a cat-lover now."

"I'm sure you could, if anyone can," thought Richard.

Over the next few days things began happening very quickly. Colonel Greenwood was implementing a great many changes to Neffertam Hall. He had called a meeting with all his employees to keep them aware of his new plans. He wanted to return some of the land back to its natural state to encourage the wildlife to return, and he was going to ensure that any spraying of crops and use of pesticides was personally approved by Richard's grandfather.

Baba was also going to be given a new title and a salary increase to go with his new responsibilities. Everyone at the meeting wondered why the

Colonel had quite such an abrupt change of attitude.

Colonel Greenwood wanted to speak to Grandpa on his own after the meeting, so he asked him to go to his study for a private chat. Apart from the Manager, the Colonel had never allowed his employees that privilege before, so Baba was intrigued and a bit nervous at this invitation. They sat down in the oak panelled room, surrounded by books, including many about the history of the hall and its owners. The Colonel offered Baba a fine crystal tumbler of Scotch whisky and motioned to one of the deeply upholstered leather armchairs in front of the huge fireplace.

"I've asked you here because I don't want anyone else to know what I am telling you now, so keep it to yourself, Oakley. D'you mind if I call you George when we're having an informal meeting, I think it would be more appropriate, don't you? You can call me Edwin if you like, but never in front of your colleagues!"

Baba was taken aback, the Colonel had never been so open or friendly with him up until today. Whatever had made him have this complete change of heart? Surely not the conference alone, successful as it was? The Colonel leaned forward conspiratorially.

"I'm pretty sure you won't believe what I am about to tell you, George. I'm not sure I understand it myself, but it seems to fit in with everything that's been happening lately. I had the most weird dream last night and I've been reliving it over and over again, and the more I think about it, the more sense it makes to me. I've checked some of the things I saw, or imagined I saw, in some of the books here. I won't relate the whole dream to you, it doesn't sound credible. To give you some idea, it was, don't laugh, a message delivered by a very large cat, wearing jewellery like those Egyptian gods of old!"

Edwin looked anxiously at George to see if he could sense any flicker of disbelief in Richard's grandfather's eyes. But no, far from it, George leaned forward and spoke as if this was a most commonplace event and completely unremarkable.

"I'm not likely to mock any dream you have with Bastet involved, Colonel. The messages you have received may chime in perfectly with events I have experienced myself, along with Katie, my daughter, and Richard, my grandson."

"Well, that's a relief. I wouldn't want you to think your employer was going potty, now would I? All right, I'll tell you what happened. This beast appeared in front of me, and at first I wasn't even aware it was a dream, it was so darned real! It looked angry, and so fierce I must say I was terrified. I've been to war and never felt so fearful.

"I'll not bore you with everything I was told but it boils down to this. I'm informed that if I don't carry out drastic changes to the way we run

this place, the consequences are likely to be disastrous. It all made perfect sense, that's why I called the meeting earlier. I am going to make certain that my orders are carried out urgently.

"However, this is the part of my dream that I want to share, and only with you. I know you've been doing research on Neffertam Hall and those who cared for it, over the many past generations. 'Bastet' I think you called the cat? Well, Bastet told me that cats were revered by the owners of the hall and that's part of the reason for its fame and success. Since this reverence ceased, the hall has deteriorated. It's become overrun with rats and mice, crops and plants have been failing despite our pesticides and land clearance operations.

"Apparently there's a place in Hathor Wood that was a shrine to cats that I've never seen. Bastet told me that you have, I believe? I want you

Mekal's casket after cleaning, ready to be replaced in the restored alcove.

to make sure it is restored to its former glory. I've found some good reference in the books here on the hall's past, some old engravings and suchlike, and I think you found some photographs in the attic that will help too? Bastet was very insistent about this, and made it clear that if we didn't act, well…"

"There might be a problem with that, Colonel. Last time we went to the crypt the bronze statue appeared to have gone from its plinth. I really don't know how we could recreate that?"

"You think there have been thieves? Well, just do your best and we shall have to hope it's enough to appease the gods, won't we? Maybe we could knock up a fibreglass replica? I'll have to think about that one…"

George didn't think that simply 'knocking up a fibreglass replica' would be at all appropriate for such an awesome beast as Bastet!

"Oh, and one more thing, George, before you go. I'm going to get some cats for the hall, it's about time we brought some more life back into the place and, though I'm really a 'dog person', I like cats enough to be happy to have a few around. It'll keep those pesky rats and mice away from nibbling the new electricity cables we've installed anyway!"

Baba went home and pondered his unusual chat with 'Edwin'. No, he'd never get used to calling Colonel Greenwood that, and couldn't imagine doing so, ever. What to do about Bastet's statue though? That's a real challenge. He would have to go and inspect the shrine deep in the woods again but knew Tolly was the only one that could find it. He would have to take Richard and his beloved cat there once more, but somehow make a record of the path taken.

Chapter Twenty-three

GOOD NEWS

Next day, Grandpa, Richard and Tolly were once more tramping through Hathor Wood. This time, apart from his torch, Baba took a pot of yellow paint and a brush, in order to mark trees at intervals along the way, so that his colleagues could find the way on their own. Occasionally they noticed broken bricks in the undergrowth. The plan was to restore the path there, so it would be easier to visit in future.

When they arrived at the mound, it all looked much the same as the last time they visited. The broken door and covering of undergrowth made a sorry sight. No wonder the cat gods were displeased. They ventured in cautiously, but everything looked unchanged: damp, dark and unwelcoming. As they approached the glass dome, Richard was first to note that the sickly yellow light that so disturbed Bastet had now reverted to soft green. The lake clean-up operation had obviously been successful.

They rounded the last bend in the tunnel and stopped transfixed. There, staring straight ahead, was the bronze figure of Bastet, seated proudly on the plinth in that unforgettable commanding pose that it had struck when they found the two lost men in the woods. No movement was apparent, so they went up to the statue and peered closely up at the head, half expecting it to speak. No, there was no sign of life, but they all felt a wonderful sense of wellbeing, as if a warm blanket of love had been thrown around their shoulders.

Tolly, who had up until now been wary of approaching the statue too closely, now jumped up onto the plinth and began to rub himself around Bastet's feet, just as he did to Richard and Katie when food or treats were around.

Richard couldn't wait to get back home to The Topiary Cat and share the good news. However, as he rightly guessed, when he came to speak to her, Bastet knew already that the bronze sculpture had returned and that the lake was now clean. Did she really know everything, Richard wondered?

"Richard, I think my tasks are all going to be carried out to my satisfaction, I have talked to the Colonel as you know and he was more receptive than I expected. I shall be going now."

"W-w-w-what?" stammered Richard, tears welling up. "You're leaving me? Please don't go…"

"Oh, Richard, I can't stay here forever, I have to return to be with the other gods."

The boy collapsed, sobbing pitifully, so noisily that Tolly came over and snuggled up to him.

"I think you misunderstand, Richard. Because of your grandfather's skill and the help you have all given me, I have imbued The Topiary Cat with the spirit of brave Tolly and some of my own wisdom. I am here on earth only to sort out some of the mess you mortals have made. My task here is finished for now, so I am leaving this leafy image behind.

"However, I want you to be aware that the gods will be watching the earth's progress very carefully from now on. I want you to think seriously about the path that you take in your own life as well. I think you are the type of human that could make others aware of the damage being caused by thoughtless and greedy mortals on your tiny blue planet. I shall return to you at some time in your life to see if you are following my guidance, for I have high hopes of you, young master.

"Of course The Topiary Cat will always be here, for I have made him into an immortal being. He will be able to keep an eye on things for me and to be another companion for you, along with your beloved Tolly."

With that, there was a strange rustling sound, and something unknowable streaked off into the sky. Almost immediately, The Topiary Cat spoke again, but this time with a different voice. Instead of the commanding tone which reminded Richard so much of his mother admonishing him, this was softer and deeper; just the way he imagined Tolly might speak, if only he could.

"Bastet has gone, Richard. I shall miss her presence but I will always be here for you and I hope you will also be here for me?"

"Oh, TTC, I was so scared you were going to leave me for ever. I couldn't bear that. Will you always be here in my garden?"

"Not all the time, Richard, I will not always be here in your grandfather's topiary. Just like you, when you go off on your own to school or on an adventure, I have things I need to do for Bastet. I will keep an eye on Mother Nature to make sure she and the cats are being suitably cared for. When you're out and about in the countryside or even on holiday, keep an eye open, for you might glimpse me in the bushes and trees around, but this is my home. I will always know if you need me, never fear."

This had all become such a rollercoaster of emotions that the boy would take some time to recover, but The Topiary Cat and Tolly reassured him that all would now be well.

His mother and grandfather soon became aware of this change in character of The Topiary Cat. They were in a sense rather relieved not to have such a very intimidating being in their own front garden, ordering them to carry out such irksome tasks, no matter how important they might be. Now they had a good and wise listener who still proffered sage advice when required, and also brought some valuable insight into the mind of Richard's beloved Russian Blue.

Tolly was profoundly changed after meeting Bastet, becoming more courageous and adventurous than ever. He became a wonderfully patient teacher of the cats now residing at Neffertam Hall and could often be seen there, sitting in the centre of a circle of his adoring students, with his paw on a captured brown rat. Every now and then he would let the rodent go and the circle of cats would part. Tolly would run after the rat and catch it again, taking it back into the ring of admirers. He was teaching them all their job and he was an exceedingly good mentor.

In fact, Tolly was supremely good at nearly all he did, apart that is from a profound weakness for chicken treats.

And Richard of course…

EPILOGUE

The Topiary Cat told Richard that some of the missions he would be asked to do might affect his whole life, and indeed they did. He became so aware of the fragility of nature and humans' lack of care for the environment that he became a lifelong supporter of efforts to minimise the impact of pollution and destruction of the natural world.

Inheriting his mother's love of painting, he also began to create images that reflected these concerns.

Katie was to become a respected artist with her Egyptian paintings being adored by collectors all over the world, while her father, Baba, lived to a ripe old age, still creating and maintaining his glorious topiaries. His restoration of Colonel Greenwood's Neffertam Hall Estate received many awards, with the Hathor Wood structures becoming a place of pilgrimage for cat lovers everywhere.

What became of Tolly? Sadly, cats are mortal but of course he lives on as the immortal Spirit of The Topiary Cat. Another Russian Blue, Georgi, came to live with Richard and his topiary alter ego, GK, now accompanies TTC on his adventures.

On the following pages you will discover half a dozen of the 'Spot the Difference' puzzles created for Facebook during the 2020 Covid-19 lockdowns. Most of them feature both topiary cats, TTC and GK. The top and bottom pictures have twelve differences between them, some easy to spot, others much harder. Look for objects that have moved, colour changes and omissions, and enjoy the hunt. The location and descriptions of the changes are on the following pages after the puzzles.

SPOT THE DIFFERENCE PUZZLE – SNOW SCENE

In this scene, just up the road from the author's home, The Topiary Cat is sleeping peacefully while Georgi Kitten, GK, dozes in the forground. Beloved Tolly walks purposefully towards us following footprints in the snow. Look for twelve differences between the top and bottom pictures.

SPOT THE DIFFERENCE PUZZLE
STATUES IN THE PARK
Opposite, Page 95

Grandpa has just completed trimming his topiary of Georgi, Richard's second Russian Blue cat. The original and 'Most Magnificent' Topiary Cat, Spirit of Tolly, ponders the foibles of mortals and the possibility of a storm approaching. Tolly echoes GK's pose in the foreground. Can you find the twelve differences between the top and bottom pictures?

The Topiary Cat

The Topiery Cat

SPOT THE DIFFERENCE PUZZLE
THE MAGICAL DOORWAY
Opposite, Page 97

What awaits the entranced visitors to this chapel devoted to The Topiary Cat? Maybe this is a portal to another world where topiary creatures rule. But will you discover twelve differences between the top and bottom pictures?

VISITORS ENTRANCED
The Topiary Cat

VISITORS ENTRANCE
The Topiary Cat

SPOT THE DIFFERENCE PUZZLE
GLAMIS CASTLE
Opposite, Page 99

The Topiary Cat and GK take a holiday to Scotland, but GK still needs his regular trim. He's not as good as TTC at keeping still but is learning from his mentor, seen sleeping peacefully camouflaged in the bushes. Tolly is on the alert for mortals who might spot movement from the topiaries, but can *you* spot the twelve differences?

The Topiary Cat

The Topiary Cat

SPOT THE DIFFERENCE PUZZLE
GOLDINGS
Opposite, Page 101

Close to home again, visiting the beautiful Goldings esate, which was once a Barnardo's home, a children's charity that protects and supports the UK's most vulnerable children and young people. This has now been developed into desirable private residences, but can you see the twelve differences between the images?

The Topiary Cat
The Topiary Cat
THE FIRST TOPIARY CAT

The Topiary Cat
The Topiary Cat
FIRST TOPIARY CAT

SPOT THE DIFFERENCE PUZZLE
THE MASTER
Opposite, Page 103

The author, posing as 'Grandpa' in front of The Topiary Cat. As you have read in the story, Bastet thinks of Richard as the 'young master' so, despite everyone knowing that mortals are merely the slaves of our feline companions, this has developed into 'The Master' as he ages. In order to keep the balance of hierarchy, The Topiary Cat is now allowed to call himself 'Most Magnificent'. There are another twelve differences for you to find here.

The Topiary Cat

The Topiary Cat

'SPOT THE DIFFERENCE' SOLUTIONS

In each of the solutions shown here, the top image of each pair is shown. Some things are added, some taken away, some moved and some change colour. On Facebook, 'The Master' is described as 'sneaky' with some of the subtle changes he has made, a description that he embraces whole-heartedly!

SNOW SCENE
page 93

1. Branch removed from in front of logo
2. Fox gone
3. Tolly moved right
4. One footprint extra
5. Less snow on GK's back
6. Shadow of tree on TTC's back gone
7. No snow on The Topiary Cat's head
8. Snow added onto topiary bush
9. East wing of building demolished
10. Branch added
11. Moon higher in sky
12. Star removed

STATUES IN THE PARK
page 95

1. Logo reads 'Topiary' not 'Topiery'
2. No 'mouse cloud'
3. Statue flipped left to right
4. Urn added over portico
5. Urn removed from plinth
6. Grandpa moved left
7. Bush removed
8. Red flowers gone
9. Georgi appeared
10. Hand position change
11. Wardrobe malfunction
12. Crook facing right

THE MAGICAL DOORWAY
page 97

1. Crook in front of TTC in window
2. Window sill added
3. Left hand topiary eye open
4. Sign over door, 'D' added
5. Stonework addition
6. Mortar complete
7. Tree added
8. Gazebo moved right
9. Hat added
10. Extra pail
11. Shadow for shears
12. Three door panels

GLAMIS CASTLE
page 99

1. Balloon higher in sky
2. Crown on top of sculpture correct way up
3. Cat on base now a lion
4. Grandpa trimming GK higher up
5. Round tower deeper
6. Window added
7. More battlements
8. Bird rotated
9. Chimney behind logo
10. Fewer pink flowers in foreground
11. Tolly flipped left to right
12. Tower removed

GOLDINGS
page 101

1. More birds in the sky
2. Lion statue moved left
3. More chimneys
4. Window removed
5. Ball topiary added
6. Larger ball topiary
7. The Topiary Cat moved left
8. Bench added
9. Colour of flowers
10. 'The' added to statue title
11. More purple flowers in foreground
12. Fewer primroses

THE MASTER
page 103

1. Hat band narrower
2. Glasses added
3. Haircut changed
4. Shirt collar down
5. Hand smaller
6. Blazer button flopped down
7. Little finger hidden
8. Logo outer ring correct colour
9. Extra leaf on logo
10. Background trees smaller
11. The Topiary Cat's ear forward
12. Branch removed

NOTES

Bastet

Bastet was originally a fierce lioness warrior goddess of the sun, worshipped throughout most of ancient Egyptian history, but later she became Bastet, the cat goddess that is familiar today. She then was depicted as the daughter of Ra and Isis. As protector of Lower Egypt, she was seen as defender of the king, and consequently of the sun god, Ra.

Along with other deities, Bastet was associated with the Eye of Ra. She has been depicted as fighting an evil snake, an enemy of Ra. In addition to her solar connections, sometimes she was called 'eye of the moon'.

Bastet was also a goddess of pregnancy and childbirth, possibly because of the fertility of the domestic cat.

Neffertam Hall

This is an Anglicised spelling of 'Nefertem'. The 'Book of the Dead' says: 'Rise like Nefertem from the blue water lily, to the nostrils of Ra, and come forth upon the horizon each day'. Nefertem was seen as the son of the creator god Ptah, and the goddesses Sekhmet or Bast his mother.

Nefertem is usually depicted as a beautiful young man having blue water-lily flowers around his head. As the son of Bastet, he also sometimes is depicted as a cat reclining. The ancient Egyptians often carried small statuettes of him as good-luck charms.

Hathor Wood

Hathor was a solar deity, a feminine counterpart to sun gods such as Horus and Ra, and was a member of the divine entourage that accompanied Ra as he sailed through the sky in his barque. She was commonly called the "Golden One", referring to the radiance of the sun.

Bastet's mound in Hathor wood has sycamores growing from it. Sycamore exists in all Egyptian districts of Delta and Upper Egypt, also in the oases. It was specifically regarded as a manifestation of the goddesses Nut, Isis and Hathor.

The Eye of Ra

The 'Eye of Ra' in Egyptian mythology functions as a feminine counterpart to the sun god Ra and as a force to subdue his enemies. The eye is an extension of Ra's power, equated with the disc of the sun, but it often behaves as an independent goddess.

This goddess is associated with several particular deities, including Hathor and Bastet. The eye goddess acts as mother, sibling, consort, and daughter of the sun god. The eye defends Ra against the agents of disorder that threaten his rule.

This dangerous aspect of the eye goddess is often represented by a lioness or cobra, a symbol of protection and royal authority, it is a prominent motif in Egyptian mythology.

Mafdet

She was a goddess in ancient Egyptian religion, often depicted wearing a skin of a cheetah and a protector against the bite of snakes and scorpions.

Mafdet was the deification of justice linked with the protection of the king's chambers and other sacred places, and with protecting the sun god Ra from venomous snakes which were seen as transgressors.

Mekal

The casket in the Hathor Wood alcove was engraved with the name of the lion goddess revered as a fierce protector strongly connected to the sun. The sun gods brought life, health and prosperity but could also be a destructive force bringing drought and pestilence.

Mekal is therefore given the title of 'Fierce Devourer'. This is why Grandpa reckoned the cat must have been a great hunter.

Silent Spring

An environmental science book by Rachel Carson.The book was published in 1962 in America and documented the adverse environmental effects caused by the indiscriminate use of synthetic pesticides. Carson accused the chemical industry of spreading disinformation, and public officials of accepting the industry's marketing claims unquestioningly.

'Silent Spring' brought environmental concerns to the public and was met with fierce opposition by chemical companies, but public opinion forced welcome changes leading to a nationwide ban on DDT for agricultural uses. In 2006, Silent Spring was named one of the 25 greatest science books of all time by the editors of Discover magazine.

The dome under the Neffertam Estate lake

The author would like to acknowledge the inspiration for the tunnel, alcoves and the glass dome under the lake at Neffertam Hall Estate. In their 1986 book 'Follies, a National Trust Guide' by Gwyn Headley & Wim Meulenkamp, on page 107/8 they describe an estate at Witley Park in Surrey, England.

Not open to the public, the authors were offered privileged access to an underground walkway illuminated by glass pavement lights set into the woodland floor. This eventually leads, via an underground flooded tunnel and a boat, to a smoking room (often described as a ballroom) under a lake similar to this author's story. It was built by Whitaker Wright, a financier and self-made millionaire.

Through reading that book in the mid-eighties, the images that were conjured up in the author's mind remain strong even now due to the impeccable writing style.

ACKNOWLEDGMENTS

I would like to thank the following individuals who provided support, encouragement, advice and, most important, proof reading for this novel. Though readers should also note that I have made various changes since the early days of writing this, so any mistakes now to be found in this printed copy are entirely my own incompetence.

Special thanks go to Helena Nash, author Jo Moss, my patient wife Janie, our daughters Emma and Allie, and my late brother Carey Saunders. I have also had much help and advice from my friends, Kevin and Viv at 'Art Van Go' and author and poet Nigel Braggins. Thanks to our daughter Alexandra Saunders for the photograph of me in the 'Spot the Difference' puzzle on page 103, under her trading name of 'Blackshield Snaps'.

I would also like to mention the unfailing support I had from so many loyal followers of The Topiary Cat on Facebook, because without them I would not have attempted this rather daunting task.

I would also like to put on record the help I had when I did a reading of this novel for SoundCloud, especially James Nicolson who edited and uploaded the files, and Lloyd Hancock who suggested this method of distribution.

Many thanks to James Sheppard-Alden for the photograph of myself in our local pub accompanying the introduction on page ii and to Robert Lane for the photograph of Glamis Castle for the 'Spot the Difference' puzzle on page 99.

Huge thanks again to James Nicolson for composing the gorgeous music and playing guitar so beautifully to accompany my YouTube videos for The Topiary Cat.

And finally, undying gratitude too, to Adam Fearn for setting up The Topiary Cat YouTube channel, plus hosting the website for The Topiary Cat and my own surrealist one, which he also created for me.

Websites: *www.thetopiarycat.co.uk* *www.surrealmoustache.co.uk*
or simply search '*The Topiary Cat*' on Google.

GOODBYE SWEET TOLLY

...and finally, as we say goodbye to our friends in Topiary Cat Land, we gaze at the wonder of the moon shining over the lake and illuminating the Most Magnificent form of The Topiary Cat, The Spirit of beloved Tolly.

Tolly himself, accompanied by Georgi Kitten gaze in awe at this immortal being while topiary GK, just out of shot, dares not intrude on this tranquil scene, knowing he would probably disrupt the peace of the occasion.

Sleep tight...